# THE CREEPY CLASSICS

## CHILDREN'S COLLECTION

Dados Internacionais de Catalogação na Publicação (CIP) de acordo com ISBD

| | |
|---|---|
| L618t | Leroux, Gaston.<br>The phanton of the opera / Gaston Leroux. - Jandira, SP : W. Books, 2025.<br>120 p. ; 12,80cm x 19,80cm. - (Classics).<br><br>ISBN: 978-65-5294-192-3<br><br>1. Literatura francesa. 2. Clássicos. 3. Fantasia. 4. Imaginação. 5. Terror.<br>6. Suspense. I. Título. II. Série |
| 2025-2532 | CDD 840<br>CDU 811.131-1 |

**Elaborada por Lucio Feitosa - CRB-8/8803**
**Índice para catálogo sistemático:**
1. Literatura francesa 840
2. Literatura francesa 821.131-1

The Creepy Classics Collection
Text © Sweet Cherry Publishing Limited, 2024
Inside illustrations © Sweet Cherry Publishing Limited, 2024
Cover illustrations © Sweet Cherry Publishing Limited, 2024

Text based on the original story by Gaston Leroux,
adapted by Gemma Barder
Illustrations by Nick Moffatt

© 2025 edition:
Ciranda Cultural Editora e Distribuidora Ltda.

1st edition in 2025
www.cirandacultural.com.br
No part of this publication may be reproduced, stored in a retrieval
system, or transmitted in any form or by any means, electronic,
mechanical, photocopying, recording, or otherwise, without written
permission of the publisher.
This book is a work of fiction. Names, characters, places, and incidents
are either the product of the author's imagination or are used fictitiously,
and any resemblance to actual persons, living or dead, business
establishments, events, or locales is entirely coincidental.

# THE PHANTOM OF THE OPERA

## GASTON LEROUX

## Mr Poligny
The Paris Opera House's retired manager

## Richard and Moncharmin
The Paris Opera House's new managers

## Raoul de Chagny
A wealthy young man and son of a viscount

## Phillipe de Chagny
Raoul's older brother

## Christine Daae
A young opera singer

# Chapter One

'The ghost! The ghost! We saw the ghost!'

A flurry of ballerinas in pink tutus rushed into the manager's office of the Paris Opera House. They were out of breath and their cheeks were flushed with fright.

'What on earth?' demanded Mr Poligny. 'Come now, ladies, please do not start with all this nonsense again, not on my last night in charge of the opera house.'

'But we saw him!' cried one of the ballerinas. 'He was in Box Five!'

Mr Poligny sighed. Most men of his age had stopped believing in ghost stories a long time ago, but most men his age had never heard of the Phantom. The ghostly being had haunted the opera house for a while, causing all kinds of annoyances and disturbances.

He knew it was quite likely that the ballerinas had seen the Phantom in Box Five, but he also knew that telling them this would scare them terribly. He only had one last performance to oversee as manager before he retired and he wanted it to go smoothly.

'Joseph the stagehand says he doesn't have a face – just a skull with red, burning eyes!' gasped another ballerina, still trembling.

'Joseph needs to keep quiet!'
hissed another. 'Mrs Giry says
the ghost doesn't like to be
talked about!'

Mr Poligny stood up and
began to wave the ballerinas
out of his office. 'That is quite
enough. Don't you all have
rehearsals to get to? I won't
hear another word about
ghosts in this opera house!'

Mr Poligny shut his door and
sat heavily on his chair. Before
the ballerinas had burst into
his office, he had been putting
together a bundle of important

papers for the new managers to look over. He had been the manager of the Paris Opera House for many years, and had overseen hundreds of wonderful operas and ballets.

Everyone in Paris longed to sit under the opera house's famous chandelier and watch the finest shows. There was one part of his job, however, that he hated having to deal with.

Slowly, Mr Poligny unlocked the bottom drawer of his desk and pulled out an envelope. His name was written in spidery handwriting on the front. Inside was a list of demands.

Sighing, he placed the list in the pile of papers, ready for the new managers. He wondered how he was going to explain to them that Box Five, one of the best seats in the theatre, was to be left empty at all times. And the reason? So that the opera house's ghost, the Phantom, would always have a place to watch the performances.

He was shaken out of his thoughts by a loud cry. He ran to the stage where a crowd of actors and theatre crew were gathered.

'What is it? What is the matter?' Mr Poligny asked.

'It's Joseph,' said one of the wardrobe mistresses, wiping a tear from her eye. 'He's dead. He's been killed! The Phantom has killed him!'

'He should never have spoken about that horrible ghost!' cried a ballerina. 'He hears everything!'

Mr Poligny pushed his way to the front of the crowd to look at the dead man. The manager's eyes darted to Box Five where he caught a glimpse of a shadowy figure. The Phantom.

# Chapter Two

Phillipe de Chagny and his younger brother Raoul loved the Paris Opera House. Being the sons of a viscount, they were given tickets for every performance. The brothers were just settling into their seats when an announcement was made.

'We are sorry to inform you that our lead opera singer, Carlotta, has

**viscount**
A nobleman of high social rank.

been taken ill. She will be replaced in this evening's performance by Christine Daae.'

'Christine Daae?' repeated Raoul, looking to his brother. 'Is that the same Christine Daae we knew when we were children?'

Raoul was a clever, well-dressed young man with the same dark hair and blue eyes as his brother.

'I believe so,' said Phillipe, frowning. 'Although I heard her family lost all their money a few years ago after the father died.

Now, she's been reduced to performing on the stage.'

Raoul rolled his eyes at his brother. 'Phillipe, being a singer is hardly a bad profession!'

'Perhaps,' Phillipe shrugged.

At that moment, the lights in the theatre dimmed. Voices hushed and the orchestra began to play.

As Christine took to the stage, Raoul leant forward. He barely recognised the little girl he used to play with. Christine had grown into a beautiful woman with long dark hair. Her singing was even more beautiful than she was. Raoul and the rest of the audience were captivated. 'Did you know she could sing so well?' Raoul whispered.

'I did not,' said Phillipe.

For the next two hours, Raoul could not take his eyes off the singer. When Christine sang the last aria of the opera, Raoul and the rest of the audience leapt to their feet. The cheering continued as Christine and the cast took a bow and the curtain fell.

Raoul suddenly felt sad that he could not see Christine anymore. 'Excuse me, brother,' Raoul said, rising from his seat. 'I might just pop backstage and say hello to Christine!' He made his way

**aría**
A song in an opera that is sung by one singer.

through the long corridors and stairways that made up the opera house until he found Christine's dressing room.

Raoul was about to knock, when he heard voices coming from inside. One was Christine's, and the other was a man's.

'I am sorry,' Raoul heard Christine say. 'You know I sing only for you.'

Raoul's heart sank. It was clear that Christine was attached to someone already. As he turned to go, the door to Christine's dressing room suddenly opened. Flustered,

Raoul hid behind a large piece of stage scenery so the singer would not see him. Christine stepped out, her face flushed and full of worry.

Filled with curiosity about who Christine was speaking to, Raoul peeked inside her dressing room. There was nobody there.

# Chapter Three

Mr Poligny was thrilled that his last night as manager of the Paris Opera House had been such a success. When Carlotta, their lead singer, had fallen ill, he was sure the night would be a disaster. Christine may not have been an experienced performer, but she had dazzled the crowd with her beautiful voice.

After the audience had left, a small party was held on the stage to say goodbye to Mr Poligny and

to welcome the new managers. Although many of the cast and crew were still shaken by Joseph's death, they had decided not to tell

Firmin Richard and Armand Moncharmin who were to take over the opera house. Richard was a small man with a cross-looking face. He knew a lot about music, but he wasn't very good at chatting with the other guests. His friend, Moncharmin, was tall and elegant. He wafted

through the party getting to know everyone, from the conductor of the orchestra to the stagehands.

'Excuse me, Mr Poligny,' said Richard impatiently. 'But haven't we got matters to discuss? We will be in charge of the opera house from tomorrow, don't forget.'

'Of course,' Mr Poligny said, a trickle of sadness filling his chest. 'Shall we go to my … I mean *your* office?'

It felt strange to Mr Poligny to be leaving the opera house after so many years, but he had to admit there was part of him that was relieved. From this night on, the Phantom would be someone else's problem. The last thing he had to do before he could retire in peace, was to make sure Richard and Moncharmin knew exactly how to keep the Phantom happy.

When most of the party guests had left, and he had gone through all the papers and handed over the keys, Mr Poligny took a deep breath and faced the new managers.

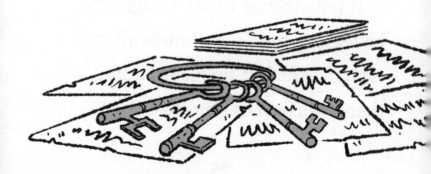

'Now, there is one last thing we need to discuss,' he said, reaching for the Phantom's list of demands. 'You may have heard stories that the opera house is haunted ...'

'Superstitious nonsense!' barked Richard.

'Oh, I don't know,' said Moncharmin, cheerfully sipping the drink he had brought with him from the party. 'All these old theatres are said to be haunted by an old grey lady or the like.'

'It is a little more complicated than that I'm afraid,' said Mr

Poligny. 'The Paris Opera House is inhabited by … the Phantom. Shortly after I started as the manager here, this list of demands appeared on my desk.' Mr Poligny handed over the worn piece of paper. 'I would strongly advise that you keep up with the Phantom's wishes.'

Richard read the paper and his face turned red with anger. 'One: Keep Box Five free at all times. Two: Pay me 25,000 francs a month … this is ridiculous! Someone has been playing a trick on you, Poligny.'

'It does seem a bit silly,' agreed Moncharmin, in a calmer voice. 'What would a ghost do with all that money anyway?' He laughed, stopping when he saw the serious look on Mr Poligny's face.

'As of tomorrow morning, the Paris Opera House is no longer my responsibility,' Mr Poligny said. 'But I am begging you to do as the Phantom wishes. You have no idea what he is capable of when he is

angry.' Mr Poligny paused for a moment, remembering the dreadful sight of Joseph's body. He thought about telling Richard and Moncharmin, but he did not want to frighten them. Richard knew a great deal about music, and Moncharmin was a wonderful businessman. They were the perfect people to manage his beloved opera house. 'The best of luck to you both.'

And with that, Mr Poligny reached for his hat and left.

# Chapter Four

Mrs Giry looked after everything that happened in front of the stage at the Paris Opera House. She helped the audience to get to their seats, made sure the auditorium was sparkling and, most importantly, she knew exactly which seats had been sold.

'Mr Richard!' Mrs Giry called after her new manager as he

### auditorium
The area in a theatre where the audience sits.

stomped through the theatre.

'What is it, Mrs Giry? Can't you see that I am busy?' Richard said. 'There has been a mistake with the ticket sales for tonight's performance,' she said. Mr Richard looked impatiently at Mrs Giry, waiting for her to explain. 'Well ... you see ... you have sold the seats in Box Five,' she said.

'Of course we have,' said Richard. 'They are the best seats in the house. People will pay a lot of money to sit in Box Five.'

'But that is the Phantom's box!' Mrs Giry said, wringing her hands with worry.

Richard sighed heavily and looked up at the ceiling in frustration. 'Mrs Giry, the Phantom is a *story*. Gossip. Nonsense! It ends now. Box Five is sold, and it will always be sold from now on!'

Mrs Giry watched as Richard's small, angry figure disappeared towards his office. She glanced back at the auditorium. It was dark as the lamps had not yet been lit inside. In the shadows, she could make out a figure in a cape, standing in the middle of the Royal Circle.

\*\*\*

Later that evening, the opera house was filled with people, excitedly chattering about that evening's performance. Richard and Moncharmin were dressed in their finest tuxedos, greeting guests and introducing themselves to the most important, richest members of the audience. With five minutes to go until the show began, Moncharmin was drawn to the sound of raised voices.

'I am sorry, sir,' he could hear Mrs Giry saying. 'I can assure you that you have the correct tickets.'

'How can that be true? There has been a mistake!' barked a man in an expensive-looking suit, his finely dressed wife next to him.

'Can I help at all?' Moncharmin said.

'You can tell me why Box Five has been double booked!' the man said. 'We have just been told, and rather rudely I might add, that Box Five is occupied!'

'Who told you this?' asked Moncharmin, as calmly as he could.

'Well, I did not see his face, I just heard his voice,' replied the man.

'It was dark inside the box and he was hiding in the shadows. He clearly did not want to be disturbed.'

Before Moncharmin could question further, Richard arrived. Mrs Giry explained the situation.

'Please accept our apologies,' said Richard, more polite than anyone had ever seen him. 'We will arrange new seats and drinks for you.'

After the angry couple had been settled in a different box, and their drinks ordered, Richard's pleasant mood vanished. 'This has to stop, right now!' he bellowed. Mrs Giry looked confused. 'I don't know what games you are playing, but this silliness will not work with me. I do not believe in ghosts or being rude to paying customers! You must have planned this somehow!'

Mrs Giry was shocked. 'But sir, I–'

'That is *it*, Mrs Giry, find your coat and leave the opera house at once,' Richard said.

Mrs Giry looked at Moncharmin for help, but the taller gentleman simply shrugged. He knew that when Richard had made up his mind, there was no point trying to change it. Mrs Giry's eyes filled with tears as she fled from the opera house.

# Chapter Five

Raoul sat in the parlour of the large, smart house he shared with Phillipe, staring at the note that had just been delivered. It was from Christine Daae.

After Raoul watched Christine's performance at the opera house, he could not stop thinking about her. The next morning, he had visited the stage door with a letter for her. Now he was holding her reply in his hands.

Thank you for coming to see me perform.
It was the best night of my life, so I
am glad you enjoyed it too! Of course,
I remember you and Phillipe. I hope your
brother is well. It would be lovely to meet
you again. Every Tuesday afternoon,
I visit my father's grave at the Père
Lachaise Cemetery. It would be lovely
to take a walk with you there.

'Good morning, brother,' said
Phillipe, entering the parlour.
'What have you got there?'
'Just a letter from an old friend,'

said Raoul. He thought it best not to tell his brother he was meeting Christine. He folded the note and placed it in his inside pocket, next to his heart, to keep it safe.

\* \* \*

The Père Lachaise Cemetery was filled with large, ornate headstones and tombs. Stone angels and cherubs lurched towards

Raoul at every turn. It seemed a strange place for a first meeting, Raoul thought. It took him a little while to find the quiet corner of the graveyard where Christine's father was buried.

'Oh!' exclaimed Christine when Raoul appeared behind her. She quickly wiped her eyes with a handkerchief.

'Excuse me, Raoul, I am feeling a little sad today.'

'Please do not apologise,' said Raoul kindly. 'I remember your father well. He was a good man and I am sure he would be very proud of you – performing at the Paris Opera House!'

Christine smiled. 'Thank you,

I hope he would be, even if the other night was my only chance to sing on that stage.'

'What do you mean? You were magnificent – surely you will be able to sing again?'

Christine shook her head. 'Carlotta is feeling much better now, and she is the main singer. She's the reason people come to the opera. It is such a shame, after all our hard work, too.'

'*Our* hard work?' Raoul said.

Christine's cheeks flushed. 'I … I shouldn't have said that,' she stuttered. 'It's just, I feel so comfortable with you – it's strange, isn't it? We haven't seen each other for years and yet I feel as though we saw each other just last week! Please, forget I said anything.'

Raoul frowned. It was clear that Christine was hiding something. Something she was scared of anyone finding out about. 'Of course, I will forget it, if that's what you wish, but I hope you know you can trust me with any secret of yours.'

Christine turned and looked at Raoul in the eyes for the first time. He was struck again by how beautiful she had become. A faint smile traced across her lips. 'Do you remember the story my father used to tell us when we were children? About the Angel of Music?'

Raoul thought for a moment. 'Why yes, I do! I remember wishing that the Angel of Music would put a spell on my fingers so that I would never have to do piano lessons again!'

Christine laughed, then took a deep breath. 'Well, I met the angel,' she said. 'That is, I know him. He has been helping me to sing better.'

## Chapter Six

Raoul was stunned. For a moment, he could only stare at Christine. 'The Angel of Music?' he repeated. 'From the fairy tale your father used to tell us?'

'It wasn't a fairy tale,' Christine said, bluntly. 'It was a true story – based on a real angel.'

'And you have met this *angel*?' Raoul said. The disbelief in his voice was clear.

'Perhaps I should not have said

anything after all.' Christine frowned, and hurried away.

'Wait!' Raoul called.

'I thought I could trust you with my secret, but clearly you don't believe me,' Christine said, not stopping to look back.

'I'm sorry,' Raoul replied, hurrying to keep up with her. 'It is a little hard to believe, but I want to. Tell me more!' But Christine shook her head and walked out of the graveyard. Raoul sighed. There was nothing for it, but to make his own way home. As Raoul turned, he caught sight of a tall figure in a

black cloak, a hat pulled down
over his face, clearly watching him.
As the figure disappeared among
the gravestones, Raoul felt a
cold wind whip round him.

\*\*\*

A few days after the incident in Box Five, a letter appeared on Richard and Moncharmin's desk. It was written in the Phantom's spidery handwriting and contained a new list of demands.

1. Christine MUST be the lead singer in the next opera, NOT Carlotta.

2. Give Mrs Giry her job back at once.

3. Do NOT attempt to sell Box Five ever again.

4. Deliver my 25,000 francs IMMEDIATELY

Do all these things, or beware ...

Richard paced around the office as Moncharmin sipped a cup of tea. 'When we took on the job as managers of the opera house, we did not agree to put up with this nonsense, this balderdash,' Richard said. 'It has gone too far!'

Moncharmin stirred a sugar into his tea. 'I agree my friend, but what are we to do about it?' he asked. 'Even the ballerinas believe the story. They are afraid that this *Phantom* will do something dreadful if we do not do as he wants.'

Richard let out a heavy sigh. 'Right. We had better go and have a word with him then,' he said, stomping out of the office.

Moncharmin was startled. He put his tea down and quickly followed. 'What do you mean? Where are you going?' he asked.

'Box Five of course,' replied Richard. 'The Phantom is so obsessed with it; it must be where we will find him.'

Richard flung open the door to Box Five and stormed inside. The plush velvet curtains and red and gold seats were undisturbed.

Richard searched each corner but found nothing. 'You see!' he said, 'Empty!'

Moncharmin folded his arms. 'I can see that,' he answered. 'But doesn't the Phantom only use the box during a performance?'

'Then we will come again, tonight,' said Richard. 'We will watch the show from this box, and Carlotta *will* be the main singer!'

# Chapter Seven

That evening, the opera house was once again filled with people, excited to see the performance. Many of the audience were disappointed that the young Christine Daae would not be the lead singer. News of her incredible voice had quickly spread around Paris.

As they had promised, Richard and Moncharmin had taken their seats in Box Five. With just a few minutes before the curtain went up, there was still no sign of the Phantom, and all in Box Five was quiet.

'You see, Moncharmin,' said Richard, rubbing his hands together with satisfaction. 'There is nothing here. The Phantom is a story, probably made up by a stagehand to get money out of us.'

Moncharmin sat back in his seat. 'You were right,' he said, still looking about the box. 'There is no one here. It remains to be seen what will happen next.'

'What an earth do you mean?'

'Well, if we have angered the Phantom, won't he do something to get his revenge?'

Richard was too angry to reply. Soon the lights had dimmed and the orchestra began playing. Carlotta strode onto the stage and took a deep breath, but when she went to sing, nothing came out but a strange, strangled croak. The audience gasped. Carlotta swallowed and took a deep breath. But yet again, only a harsh-sounding croak escaped. Each time she tried to sing, she sounded like a toad. Carlotta ran from the stage in tears clutching her throat. The orchestra stopped playing and the conductor looked up to Box Five, waiting for instructions on what to do next.

'It's the Phantom,' said Moncharmin, calmly.

'It is NOT!' said Richard.

At that moment, a loud crack came from the ceiling. All eyes were drawn to the huge, glittering chandelier that hung from the auditorium's roof. 'It's going to fall!' shouted someone in the

audience, as the light-fitting began to shake and sway. The audience scrambled out of their seats, screaming and shouting as, with another loud crack, the chandelier hurtled towards the ground.

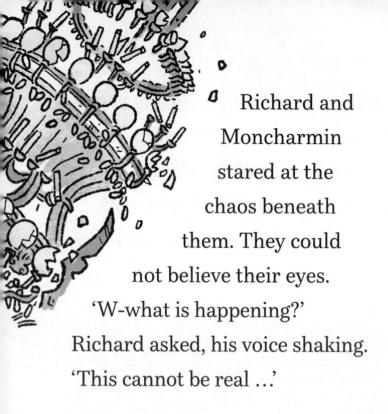

Richard and Moncharmin stared at the chaos beneath them. They could not believe their eyes.

'W-what is happening?' Richard asked, his voice shaking. 'This cannot be real …'

# Chapter Eight

When Raoul heard of the accident at the opera house his first thought was of Christine. Although she was not the lead singer, she was still in the performance and would have seen everything. He rushed to the opera house at once.

'I'm afraid she's not here,' said the conductor, sticking his head out of the stage door. 'Any further performances have been cancelled until we can get the chandelier fixed.

Have you tried her house? She lives with her grandmother.' The conductor scribbled the address on a ticket stub and handed it to Raoul who thanked him.

When Raoul arrived at Christine's grandmother's house, he could see how far her family had fallen. The street was lined with small, cramped houses. Many of the windows were boarded up. Raoul knocked gently and the door was answered by a tiny old woman who beckoned him inside into a small but well-kept kitchen.

'You want to see Christine?' she asked, smiling through gappy teeth.

'If I may,' replied Raoul, politely. 'Is she here?'

'Oh no, no, no, Christine is almost never here!'

'Do you know where I might find her?'

Christine's grandmother's eyes sparkled and her grin widened. 'She is with the Angel of Music!' she said, happily.

Raoul sighed. *Not this again*, he thought.

'I can see you don't believe me,' said the old woman, waggling a long, bony finger at him. 'You young men have no imagination. But without the angel, Christine would not be where she is today. He has helped her so much.'

'How has he helped her?' Raoul asked. He needed to know everything about this angel to discover who he really was.

'He has taught her how to use her voice.'

'But, *who* is he?'

'All I know is that he lives in the Paris Opera House. It is his opera house really. He controls everything that happens there.'

Raoul suddenly remembered the tall, shadowy figure in the black cloak who had been watching him at the graveyard. Did he have something to do with this? Worry bubbled in Raoul's stomach. Who was the angel, and what did he want with Christine? The only thing that Raoul knew for certain was that he had to find out.

# Chapter Nine

A week passed by and Raoul heard nothing from Christine. The opera house was closed for repairs, and every time he visited Christine's home, her grandmother gave him the same story: Christine was with the Angel of Music.

As the days went by, Raoul grew more and more frustrated. He could not talk to Phillipe about his fears. His brother had made it very clear that he did not think Christine was a suitable person for Raoul to be spending time with. The de Chagny brothers were not meant to fall in love with *singers*.

'Brother!' Phillipe said, bursting into Raoul's bedroom one afternoon. He was wearing a mask over his eyes and nose and it was covered in bright red feathers.

'What *are* you wearing?' Raoul laughed, quickly hiding the note he had been writing to Christine.

'Don't tell me you have forgotten?' Phillipe sighed. 'We have been invited to a masked ball at the opera house. The new managers are holding it to raise money for repairs to the chandelier. We got the invitation days ago.'

Raoul shrugged as Phillipe tossed a pile of post onto his bed, the invitation on top.

'Then it's a good job I bought this for you!' Phillipe said, handing Raoul a mask just like his, but with green feathers. 'I thought it would go well with your green suit. Now hurry! We leave in thirty minutes.'

Raoul put the mask onto his bed. The last thing he felt like doing was going to a fundraising party. He flipped lazily through the post until he suddenly spotted some handwriting he recognised. A letter from Christine!

Dearest Raoul,

I am sorry for walking away from you the other day at the graveyard. I loved seeing you again, truly. Perhaps we can talk again at the masked ball? I have been invited as I am now the main singer at the opera house. Carlotta's voice has still not recovered after that dreadful night. I am sorry for her, but it means you and I can see each other again at last!

Sent with love,
Christine

Raoul's heart leapt. Christine *had* been in touch and she wanted to see him! All of his moping had meant he had almost missed her message! It was all he had hoped for. He had so many questions for her, but right now it was enough that she was thinking about him.

\*\*\*

Richard and Moncharmin had transformed the opera house's stage and auditorium into a beautiful ballroom. They knew they had to do something spectacular to stop the gossip that was flying around Paris. Almost as soon as the chandelier had hit the ground, whispers had begun that the Phantom was to blame. They were delighted to see the theatre filled with rich, masked guests, ready to make large donations for the repair of the grand chandelier.

As soon as Raoul arrived at the ball, he could only think of finding one person, and one person only. Soon enough, he spotted her.

## Chapter Ten

Despite the fact that Christine was wearing a white mask over her eyes, Raoul would recognise her anywhere. He weaved his way through the crowd of people and lifted his mask a little as he greeted her.

'Raoul! I am so glad you came. I was not sure you would,' Christine said.

'I have called at your house every day. Your grandmother told me you were …' Raoul hesitated. Saying the words 'Angel of Music' made him feel foolish.

Christine looked down. 'She told you I was with the Angel of Music,' she said quietly. 'Oh Raoul, I have been so silly. I want to explain everything to you, but …'

Suddenly, Christine gasped and grabbed hold of Raoul's arm. Her eyes were fixed on something behind him. Turning, Raoul saw a tall figure half hidden behind a curtain. Party guests swirled around him, but Raoul was certain – it was the same person he had seen in the graveyard. He was wearing the same black cloak and hat and had a white mask that covered the left side of his face.

'Who is that?' Raoul demanded. Christine looked frightened, her hand still clasped onto his arm. 'Is that the man who calls himself the Angel of Music? Let me speak to him.'

'No!' Christine cried, blocking Raoul's path, as the shadowy figure disappeared in the crowd.

Raoul looked at Christine. She was trembling and her eyes glistened with tears. 'What hold does that man have over you?' Raoul asked. He lowered his voice. 'Talk to me, Christine, please let me help you!'

Christine shook her head as tears began to fall. 'No one can help me, it is too dangerous! I can't let him hurt you, you are too sweet and kind. I am sorry, Raoul, you should forget about me!' With that, she ran off among the crowd.

'Christine!' Raoul cried. He tried to follow her, but his path was blocked by a man he had never met before.

'Excuse me, sir, I must speak to you,' the stranger said. It was clear from his accent that he was not from Paris. Raoul tried to step past him, but he was blocked once again. 'I must insist ... I know who you are chasing and I can help. My name is Daroga and I–'

'I'm sorry, I have no time to talk to you,' Raoul cried. All he cared about was finding Christine.

Raoul ran through the twisting corridors of the opera house to Christine's dressing room. As he

pushed open the door his ears were filled with a beautiful male voice, though there was no one else in the room but Christine. She stood, trance-like, in front of her long, dressing mirror. As Raoul watched, Christine took a step forward and disappeared through the mirror.

# Chapter Eleven

Raoul did not sleep at all that night. He could not tell Phillipe what he had seen. His brother would not believe him, Raoul could barely believe it himself. Christine had stepped *inside* a mirror and completely disappeared. Raoul had tried everything, banging the mirror and calling her name, but he could not follow her through.

Bleary eyed and wild with worry, Raoul made his way back to the opera house the next morning. It was only then he remembered the man who had tried to talk to him at the party. Daroga. It was an odd name. Did he really know who the Angel of Music was?

The auditorium was dark and still. The glittering decorations from last night's ball had been cleared away and there was a chill in the air. When Raoul got to Christine's dressing room, he found her curled up on a chair.

'Raoul!' she said leaping up and running into his arms. 'I am so glad that you are here.'

'What happened?' Raoul said, hugging her tightly. 'I came to your room and I saw you vanish. Through that …!'

He pointed at the mirror. Christine pulled away and glanced at it fearfully. 'I want to tell you everything, but not here. We must go somewhere he can't hear us!' She grabbed Raoul's arm and led him through the theatre. They climbed up past the seats at the very top of the theatre, past the lighting rig and up through a trapdoor onto the roof.

'Isn't it beautiful?' Christine said, looking out at the view as the sun rose over Paris. 'This is the only place I can escape.'

Raoul tore his eyes away from the view. 'Escape from what?'

'It's time I told you everything' Christine said, taking a deep breath. 'When my father died, he promised me an angel would look after me.

When I started at the opera house, I heard tales of the mysterious Phantom who caused trouble around the opera house, but I kept to myself. One day, I heard a beautiful voice singing to me before a performance. I asked the voice if he was the Angel of Music. He sang back, saying that he was. He appeared to me one night through the mirror, his face covered by a strange, white mask. He taught me to sing as beautifully as he did.

When our stagehand Joseph was found dead, everyone in the theatre blamed the Phantom, a silly ghost story, but it was then that I began to think that the angel and the Phantom were the same person.

When I took Carlotta's place that night at the opera, I thought he would be pleased, but he flew into a jealous rage. He made me promise that I was singing just for him! It got worse when he saw you at the graveyard. He forbade me from seeing you ever again. He said that if I spoke to you, terrible things would happen to you. Then, there was the dreadful evening at the opera. Carlotta's voice was ruined – I can't be sure, but I have a feeling the Phantom caused it to happen. And then the chandelier!' Christine covered her face with her hands.

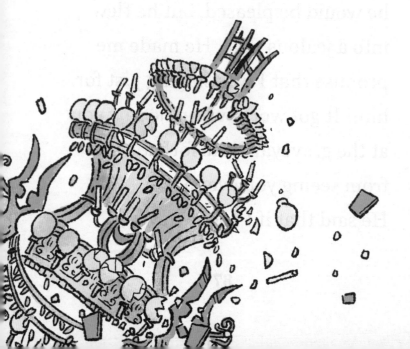

# Chapter Twelve

Christine took a shuddery breath. 'I was terrified of what the Phantom might do next,' she continued. 'But I had to spend each day with him, to try and make him feel better. I didn't want him to cause any more harm. Then, Richard and Moncharmin announced they were going to hold a masked ball to raise money to buy a new chandelier and I knew that would be the only chance

I would have to speak to you!'

'Then I ruined your plan by asking you so many questions,' Raoul said. 'I didn't let you speak. I am so sorry, Christine.'

'I knew as soon as the Phantom had seen you that he would be angrier than he ever has been before. He took me to his secret lair, hidden beneath the opera house. There are dozens of hidden tunnels and passageways all over and under the theatre. That's how he gets to Box Five without being seen.'

'So, he's not a ghost at all then?'

Raoul smiled a little. 'Or an angel?'

Christine blushed. 'No, I can't believe I ever thought he was an angel. I think he is badly scarred under his mask. It makes him feel as though he should hide away. He was very lonely, but he is not a good person. He lied to me about being the Angel of Music and he killed Joseph because he talked badly about him! He is dangerous!' She took another deep breath. 'But Raoul, I have promised never to leave him if he leaves you alone, I could not bear it if the same thing happened to you.'

Raoul felt his heart fill with joy and break in two at the same moment. Christine cared about him, and he cared for her, but she was being trapped by a horrible man. 'There must be something we can do,' he said.

Suddenly, a piercing cry filled the air, like a wounded animal trapped and in pain. As it faded, Raoul and Christine clung to each other in fear. 'It was him!' Christine said. 'He must have heard everything!'

Raoul grabbed Christine's hand. 'You must come with me, now,' he said, pulling her back towards the trapdoor which led back down into the theatre. 'We must tell someone about all this and get that man arrested!'

'No!' cried Christine. 'If I leave, he will only come for you. I made a promise not to leave the opera house. And who would believe us? Everyone knows the stories of the ghost that haunts the opera house, and no one will want to anger him!'

Raoul shook his head. 'I will find a way to come and get you, Christine. I promise.'

# Chapter Thirteen

A few nights later, the opera house opened again to unveil the newly repaired chandelier. A performance was held, with Christine as the lead singer. Carlotta's voice had still not returned.

Raoul and Phillipe took their usual seats. 'You look nervous tonight, brother,' said Phillipe, noticing how Raoul's eyes darted around the theatre.

'I am fine, Phillipe,' Raoul replied. 'I am looking forward to seeing Christine.'

His brother scoffed but Raoul ignored him. Right now, Phillipe was the least of his worries.

Once again, the lights dimmed, and the theatre fell silent as the performance began. Christine stepped out on stage wearing a white dress and a long white cloak. She began to sing, and the audience were captivated by her beautiful voice. Suddenly, as Christine reached the end of her song, the auditorium was plunged into darkness. Moments later, the lights came on again, but Christine had vanished.

Raoul jumped from his seat and ran onto the stage. 'Where is she?' he cried, looking at the other performers. 'Where is she?' But no one could tell him. It was as though she had disappeared into thin air. Raoul ran to Christine's dressing room. His heart sank when he saw that it was empty. He banged on her long mirror and shouted through the glass. 'Christine!'

'Perhaps I might be of some help?' said a voice behind him.

# Chapter Fourteen

A tall, thin man with black hair was standing in the doorway to Christine's dressing room. It was Daroga, the same man who had tried to speak to Raoul at the masked ball. 'I believe we are chasing the same person,' he said.

'You know the Phantom?' Raoul asked.

'Yes, but I know him by his real name – Erik. I have known him for many years, but the first time

I met him he was working for the circus in Persia, my home country.'

'Do you know where he has taken Christine?' Raoul asked, desperately.

Daroga stepped in front of the mirror. He felt along the outside ridge of the frame and smiled. Raoul heard a faint click, and the glass swung away from them to reveal a secret passage.

'It is one of Erik's many tricks,' Daroga said. 'Erik was a gifted singer and also created incredible

### circus
A travelling show with a variety of dancing, singing and and performing acts.

magic tricks for the circus, but he could be cruel and jealous. I have always tried to help him, but now he has gone too far. I want to stop him from hurting anyone else – or himself – again.'

Daroga walked into the passageway and beckoned for Raoul to follow.

'Why haven't you told anyone about this before now?' Raoul asked. 'If you knew how bad the Phan– I mean, Erik, was?'

Daroga shook his head. 'I wanted to give Erik a chance to rebuild his life. The last I heard about him was many, many years ago. He had been hired to work on building the Paris Opera House, so I thought he was going up in the world,' Daroga explained. 'Then I started to hear stories about a ghost in the walls of the opera house. Of strange happenings and recently, the death of a stagehand. I knew I had to act, and managed to get an invitation to the ball. I thought I would be able to find him and talk sense into him. When I saw how you reacted, I was certain you wanted to find him, too.'

'But why is he like this?' Raoul asked.

'Erik has not had an easy life. His face was badly scarred at birth and he never let anyone get close to him. He wears his white mask to hide the scars, but people stare at that even more. It has made him bitter and angry at the world.'

The dark, damp tunnels seemed to go on for ever. 'How do you know where you are going?' asked Raoul.

'I know Erik's tricks and the way his mind works. I have managed to slip into the opera house a couple of times without him seeing me. The more I know about what he is up to, the better I can help him and stop him from hurting anyone else.'

Finally, they reached a door with a heavy metal lock. Daroga pulled a small pin from his pocket and skilfully picked the lock. The door opened to reveal a room filled with mirrors.

# Chapter Fifteen

Daroga nodded his head at the mirrors. 'This was one of Erik's finest tricks when he worked at the circus. The room is designed to make whoever is inside feel uncomfortable and lost.'

'Then why have you brought *me* here?' Raoul asked suspiciously. Who was to say Daroga was not working with the Phantom as they had known each other for so long.

'I suspect this room is next to Erik's living quarters. He must be keeping Christine nearby,' Daroga said, quietly.

Raoul and Daroga pressed their ears against the wall. Soon they began to hear voices.

'I did not want to do this, Christine!' said an older-sounding male voice. 'It could all be so easy! I want a simple life. A wife, children, a home. We could have it all! But you must decide this evening. I will not wait any longer.

If you marry me, we can leave Paris tonight. If you don't, I will deal with Raoul the same way I dealt with Joseph. Either way, you are headed for church – it is up to you whether you attend a wedding or a funeral!'

'He is holding her captive!'

### captive
When someone is kept a prisoner or kept in a space that they cannot escape.

whispered Raoul. 'We need to save her!'

'It is not as simple as that,' Daroga answered. 'Christine has spent months with Erik. He has taught her how to use her voice and now he feels as though she belongs to him. Erik is not stable. We must be careful.'

A door slammed, and Christine's sobs echoed through the wall. 'It sounds as though she is alone,' Daroga whispered.

'Christine!' Raoul called, his mouth against the wall.

'Raoul, is that you?' Christine

replied. She sounded astonished. 'How did you find me?'

'I have had help from ...' Raoul looked at Daroga who shook his head and placed a finger to his lips. '... a friend.'

'It is better that Erik does not know I am here,' said Daroga.

'He has locked the door and tied me to a chair!' said Christine. 'But I think I can make it to the spare set of keys he keeps by the door.'

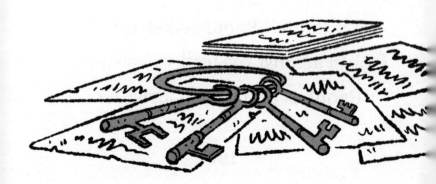

Raoul and Daroga heard what sounded like a chair scrape across the floor, followed by a loud clatter.

'I've got them!' Christine said. 'Wait, I think he is coming back!'

Raoul pressed his face closer to the wall, determined to hear everything.

'Well, have you made your decision?' Erik said.

There was no reply from Christine.

'Have you been trying to free yourself? Why are you so desperate to leave me? Don't you realise you are *mine* to control?'

Raoul could not stand to hear any more. He cried out, thumping the wall.

'What was that?' came Erik's voice. There was the sound of footsteps. 'Of course. The young hero has come to rescue you. Well, let's see about that ...'

# Chapter Sixteen

Light suddenly filled the mirror room, reflecting off every surface. Raoul and Daroga winced, shielding their eyes against the glare.

'What is happening?' cried Raoul. 'I can't see!'

'This is what the mirror room was designed for,' Daroga said. 'Light bounces off every mirror until you can't see anything.'

Suddenly, they heard the sound of water surging towards them.

On the other side of the wall, Erik looked at Christine and laughed. 'You see, Christine. Nothing will stop us from being together. Not those pathetic men who call themselves *managers*, not

young men who say they love you but do not know the meaning of the word. Not anything or anyone!'

'Please stop it!' Christine begged, tears streaming down her face. 'I beg of you, do not let him drown. I will do anything, I will marry you!'

'You will?'

'Yes! Please, just stop the water, I am begging you!'

Erik strode over to the corner of the room and pulled a lever towards him. The sound of the rushing water stopped. Christine shut her eyes in relief as she

realised that Raoul was safe.
On the other side of the wall,
the water stopped flowing and the
blinding light disappeared. Raoul
and Daroga were left dazed as the
water swirled around their chests.

She felt the ties that bound her
to her chair loosen.

'I am sorry,' Erik whispered.
'I am so very sorry.'

Christine opened her eyes and
for the first time really saw Erik –
not the Phantom, or the Angel of
Music, but just a man. His white
mask had slipped, and she could
see some of the scarring that

lay underneath. With a shaking hand, she stroked his hair and took off his mask. She placed her hand on his scars. He was just a man after all. A man who had been given so little love in his life that his mind had twisted him into a monster.

Erik looked at her in shock. No one had ever touched his

scars before. He had always been afraid to let anyone in. But now, Christine was showing him kindness even after all the terrible things he had done. Suddenly, he knew what he had to do. He smiled at her, squeezing her hand one last time. 'Go,' he said, so quietly that Christine was unsure she had heard him correctly. 'Go!' Erik said again. 'I set you free.'

Christine stood up and looked at the open door behind Erik. 'Thank you!' she said, turning for one last time before she ran. 'Thank you.'

# Epilogue

Christine De Chagny was getting ready in her dressing room, a big bouquet of flowers from her husband, Raoul, sat next to her. That night's performance was sold out, as it had been for many weeks. She glanced at the long mirror, remembering for a moment the events of last year. She had not seen Erik since that terrifying day, and the strange happenings at the Paris Opera House had

stopped – much to Richard and Moncharmin's relief.

As Christine stepped on stage her eyes wandered to Box Five. It was filled with well-dressed people, eagerly waiting for the show to begin. She took a deep breath, and began to sing.

## AUTHOR BIOGRAPHY
# GASTON LEROUX

Gaston Leroux was born in Paris in 1868. He worked as a journalist and theatre critic, and he also wrote detective fiction. Leroux read about a fire at an opera house that had caused a counterweight for a chandelier to crash through the ceiling. This and rumours of a ghost inspired him to write *The Phantom of the Opera*. The success of the novel led to several film and stage adaptions.